Easter Island

Aaron Blair

"Easter Island," by Aaron Blair. ISBN 1-58939-119-5 (softcover); 1-58939-118-7 (electronic version).

Published 2001 by Virtualbookworm.com Publishing Inc., P.O. Box 9949, College Station, TX , 77842, US. ©2001 Aaron Blair. All rights reserved. No part of this publication may be reproduced, stored in a retrieval system, or transmitted in any form or by any means, electronic, mechanical, recording or otherwise, without the prior written permission of Aaron Blair.

Manufactured in the United States of America.

Easter Island

Chapter 1

I can't remember how long I had been there. There is something about monotony that blends days together. I went there, much like everyone else, in hope of a better life. A better life! Funny to look back on it all now but that was what we were promised.

The situation had got pretty bad back home. Our technology finally surpassed any efforts that Mother Nature made to maintain the inhabitability of Earth. Disease was all but wiped out by modern medicine, child mortality was up, and it seemed that there wasn't anything that a doctor couldn't fix. We were told it was an achievement, but didn't realize that all that we had worked towards would ultimately lead to our downfall.

The animals were the first sign. Extinction was happening at an alarming rate, everyday we were losing a different species. Not the domesticated, or mass produced animals, but animals like Lions, Bears, I guess anything that couldn't live in direct contact or serve some purpose for humanity had to go. The efforts of organizations like Greenpeace did not go unnoticed, we all felt bad, we all agreed that something should be done and hoped that someone would do something. After awhile Greenpeace had nothing to fight for because the animals were gone, and without our conscience, Greenpeace, speaking, mankind could finally finish what they had started. In hindsight I always think of an article I read long ago. It was in some science magazine that talked about Easter Island.

Easter Island was best known as one of the eight wonders of the world. It is a desolate island that has huge heads carved of stone scattered throughout the landscape. The mystery was: how did these huge stone heads get on this desolate island? The various theories of aliens, giants, etc. were thrown about, but leave it scientists to dispel any wonder or magic from a perfectly good mystery.

According to the article Easter Island was inhabited by a group of Polynesians that had migrated there by boat around 500 CE. What they found was a tropical paradise, one that resembled Hawaii in the twentieth century. The island contained every thing that the tribe could want or need. At the height of their success the tribe's population grew into tens of thousands, which is an astronomical number considering the time and the size of the island! That was when the trouble began.

A rich tribe member, or so the article stated, that as a show of his great power he decided to erect one of these monoliths. Humanities' big head had reared its ugly face, so to speak, and human nature took over. Every wealthy tribe member decided that they had to erect a monolith as well, one that was even bigger than that of their neighbors. The larger the head the greater their superiority. Because of their limited technology scientists concluded that it took roughly thirty trees to move and erect these stone monuments. The island had hundreds of the stone monoliths that vary in size, most of which can still be seen. Because the monoliths required so many trees to erect them, the trees eventually disappeared. The domino effect began.

Once the trees were gone the birds that would migrate there disappeared. There were no more trees to build canoes so fishing suffered. Eventually all the coastal fish, the fish that were accessible, disappeared because the natives were consuming them faster than they could replenish their population. The tribe had no means of escaping the island because it was located in the middle of the Pacific Ocean and they had no trees to build boats. The tragedy had just begun.

The political structure collapsed and anarchy ensued. People resorted to cannibalism for food and were doomed for extinction until they were discovered by an English explorer who rescued the remaining hundred or so inhabitants. Scientists came to this conclusion by excavating ancient hearths where human remains were found.

It must have been a horrifying experience being a tribesman watching your civilization decay into chaos. I always wondered if the people knew that their situation was self-inflicted or if they thought it was due to some punishment of the gods. Yes the natives must have pondered that thought while chewing on their neighbor. They could be proud though, the natives, they provided a world with a mystery and built something that would far outlast their civilization, that is the goal of life after all isn't it, to leave behind a legacy. I always thought the story of Easter Island proved that kindness is not human nature, competitiveness and greed are the natural inhabitants of the human soul.

I think of that story often, it's why I went there. I look at Easter Island as the story of Earth writ small. The people of Easter Island destroyed their land because of their own vanity, and had no escape from their Island to save their civilization. The people of Earth were much the same they drove fast cars, ate fast food, they worked hard so they could get to the top as fast as they could. All this so they could buy faster cars, and bigger houses than their friends, siblings, and co-workers. The inhabitants of Earth were faced with the same dilemma. Where could they go once the Earth was uninhabitable? Unlike the inhabitants of Easter Island we had the scientists, ones that could foresee that the Earth was doomed to a similar fate, and humanity would follow if an alternate plan were not created. That's where I came in.

NASA has always been portrayed as a romantic organization. One committed to the exploration of the universe. Maybe they were when we were young and naïve. However, later NASA became a corporate puppet that was designed to find alternatives to the population problem that Earth faced. It's funny how that sounds. There were hundreds of different conspiracy shows that seemed so ludicrous and made us embarrassed to make those kinds of accusations. So embarrassed that no one would make any accusations. The characters in those shows were portrayed as insane, idiotic, or ludicrous. By portraying characters in that way none of us wanted to be labeled as one of those people, so we kept our thoughts to ourselves. At the end of the day NASA was built to colonize. It shouldn't have come as a big surprise. Neil Armstrong took the Moon in the name of the American people by planting America' s major export, garbage, a plastic flag, on the surface. It was mid twenty-first century when They began to contact people with "the opportunity of a lifetime". I took that call and the opportunity.

They targeted people without family, without success, and without hope. We were offered millions annually to contribute to the preservation of mankind. We were heroes, well paid heroes. Not one of us could refuse. I thought I was being rescued from my pit of despair. I was working odd jobs, lonely, friendless, not knowing what I wanted out of life. I was beginning to believe that there was nothing on Earth to live for, so what better opportunity than one to leave my burden behind and start fresh, with a wad of cash to boot.

Mars had to be manipulated by humans before it could be inhabited. The difficulties that needed to be overcome were the atmosphere, agriculture, and maintaining the conditions that made life possible. Mars' atmosphere was very thin, something that was happening to the Earth's atmosphere at the time of our mission. The problem was that Mars' atmosphere was largely composed of Carbon Dioxide. This wasn't all bad news Carbon Dioxide is what trees require to produce oxygen. However, trees also need water to survive, a certain temperature, etc. Mars could not offer these conditions so humans had to create them. First humans had to create the greenhouse effect. A notion I remember having such negative connotations during the twentieth century, but the greenhouse effect is required for human existence. Mars already had the greenhouse effect present in its atmosphere, but it only made the temperature fluctuate around five-degrees. With the average temperature on Mars' surface being roughly minus fifty degrees Celsius we needed to pump Mars' atmosphere with greenhouse producing agents to raise the temperature. This was accomplished by bombarding Mars' surface with bombs that contained greenhouse producing agents like, Methane, Nitrous Oxide, Chlorofluorocarbons, Hydrofluourocarbons, and Perfluorocarbons, the latter three were more commonly known as CFCs, HFCs, and PFCs in the late twentieth century.

Raising the temperature was not the only thing needed to make Mars inhabitable, water was also required otherwise the trees would not be able to produce oxygen. By making the surface temperature of Mars an average of ten degrees Celsius we were able to make use of water without it freezing. However Mars was not well suited to sustain water. The surface was dry and lacked any tectonics. This means that the water flow could not be sustained. That is where we came in.

It was our responsibility to create a complex irrigation system by drilling into the hard crust of Mars' surface. This would enable a direct flow of water to the trees that would be planted after the channels had been dug. The trees would get water, the surface was warm enough for life, and the trees would return our favor to them by releasing oxygen and moisture into the atmosphere for us. Mars would also have to have a method of producing water for the trees because the water would be absorbed by the surface without the presence of tectonics. Another dilemma to be considered was that there were no volcanoes to replenish the atmosphere of Mars. This was not our concern. We were sent to Mars to dig the irrigation system. That was going to be our price of glory and fame.

We, the proud few, underwent an extensive training program. All heterosexual men, the presence of both sexes would just provide the fuel that might ignite those messy human relationships, at least that was Their thinking. It was difficult, much like what boot camp was like for soldiers I imagine. Except for the plastic tubes and the ungodly locations they found to stick them.

We all finished the program and were sent to our destination without any media play or fanfare, I guess that was to be left for those who would take credit for our accomplishments once our work was done. We arrived on Mars afraid, regretful, and curious. We were forced to settle in quickly, and work began immediately. The bonds that were tied during our training were broken quickly.

We worked in suits that were identical to each other and we couldn't hear each other talk. Each suit was a cell. A cell designed to isolate us from each other. In hindsight this was probably Their idea to ensure that there could be no individuality, no communication between each other, no bonding, and ultimately no revolution, which is what They were probably most afraid of. No one could know whom one was attempting to communicate with and after awhile no one cared. The one hope that remained was with all the money that we were being paid. The belief was that eventually we could retire and enjoy the fruits of our labor back home on Earth. However, They didn't overlook anything. We were paid in the millions but simple things like food, cost thousands, tens of thousands of dollars. It was the importing costs they told us.

Our spirits were completely broken we weren't building a nest egg we were poor, lonely, and trapped. There was no alternative, no escape. We were slaves. I remember one day that someone tried to resist by refusing to work. He was beaten for all of us to see. He was beaten viciously. He was made an example of. There were no witnesses who could hear our cries or see the atrocities that were being committed. We were alone. There was no injustice being done, because it takes witnesses to realize an injustice.

Easter Island

    The situation was not completely hopeless, though it may have seemed so at the time. After all I am now able to relate our chronicles to an audience. There usually is a catalyst of some kind, a catalyst that drastically changes your fortunes. My catalyst occurred in a matter of fact kind of way. I remember the day because it knocked me off my feet, literally. I'd like to say it was a dark and stormy night, for effect, but the truth is that all the days were the same. The planet did not really have weather, except for a dust storm here and there.

Easter Island

Chapter 2

I was working the land with my state of the art equipment. My muscles had given up long ago trying to wrestle my metal foe. I learned to surrender to the motion of the machine. That day my trusty companion seized. It reminded me why I used to wrestle with my sidekick. I never trusted technology. That was the first time my machine ever betrayed my trust. I was thrown for a nasty spill. Covered in dust I leaped to my feet. I shook off the shock, and after cursing that incredulous machine that I trusted with all my heart, I decided to investigate the cause of the sudden change in its attitude.

Upon inspection of the sharp spikes that tear at the skin of the planet I found a chip, not a chip in the spike, a chip of stone. It was unlike any stone I had ever seen on the planet since my arrival. I was excited, so unnaturally excited that it seems quite ludicrous now. A grown man gleefully jumping about holding a stone chip to the sky with pride. I was not far from frolicking, which should illustrate the cabin fever I must have been suffering from at the time. I wanted to get the attention of one of my fellow workers so I could share my find. I scanned the area but could see no one. They kept us separated when we worked.

I spotted a worker in the distance and rushed as fast as I could to his spot. It was odd rushing up to him; it was like I was running toward a mirror, all of us were in identical attire. Faceless drones working diligently for the queen. I hoped with all my heart that when I had reached this replica that it wouldn't be me, which at this point I half believed could be possible. The man noticed me when I got to within a hundred yards of him. He jumped, my approaching him was highly irregular and one couldn't help but be constantly on edge when in the field. Irregularity typically meant trouble. He armed himself with his metallic friend brandishing it like a swashbuckler brandishes his sword. I stopped dead in my tracks realizing the danger of the situation. I couldn't communicate with him because he couldn't hear anything I would say, and he would've killed me if I approached him before I could communicate that I was on a mission of peace.

Luckily seeing my reaction to his show of aggression banished any thoughts of danger he was experiencing. He cautiously approached me to investigate what had happened to me that was so important that I risked my life to reach him. Realizing that we couldn't actually speak to each other we started gesticulating to each other flailing limbs in an attempt to communicate with each other. We must have looked pretty silly two grown men flapping their arms looking like they were trying to fly. This is what our highly evolved species had come to in the communication department. After numerous games of charades, those excruciating days at camp did pay off; I was able to communicate to my new-found friend what had happened. We came to an agreement to meet at my abode, after our work had been completed that day. I drew a map in the dust of where my home was located from our current location. We parted company and returned to the field knowing that we were to meet later.

The rest of the day I couldn't focus on work. My mind was racing with possibilities. My excitement did not stem from my findings as much as I was going to have my first guest since I had arrived so long ago.

The houses that we were provided with didn't resemble the houses back home. They were like hives. Hives were appropriate because they resembled a rash on the skin of our new home. A disease that we were bound to inflict on Mars, just like we had done to Earth. The hives had no windows. That was all right because there was nothing to see anyway, nothing that we wanted to see at any rate. The hives all were equipped with an artificial environment that warmed us and pumped out stale air so that we could survive without having to constantly wear our suits.

I prepared two meat rations, this was, after all, a special occasion, and it wouldn't be hard for me to skip dinner for a day. I would have to because we were never given more than what was needed to survive on a weekly basis. I awaited with anticipation my first dinner guest. I couldn't help but wonder who it would be. Mark Devon from boot camp, or maybe Tarick Williams I had a good relationship with both of them. I was afraid that I wouldn't be able to recognize who it would be, or likewise for my visitor.

The time had come and my companion entered my humble abode. It startled me it was the first time the door to my hive had ever opened without me exiting or entering. All the doors were equipped with motion sensors keys were not required because there was nothing to steal or keep safe. The cold indistinguishable suit walked in and my heart leaped as I realized that it could've been one of Them who could kill me on the spot. I rose to my feet to meet my fate if at all ill. I welcomed death, escape, and was invigorated. It was like Xmas from my childhood, this man was the gift, his suit the wrapping, underneath was my fate, and I couldn't wait.

After entering the inner door of my hut, there was a door to the hive located on the outer shell and an inner door to protect us from asphyxiation if the door to the hive ever opened erroneously, the man took off his headpiece. It came off slowly and as each feature revealed its self I tried to make out who it was. After the headpiece was fully removed I still was guessing, I didn't know this person, it must have been one of Them. I braced myself for death. My dinner guest recognizing my reaction to his appearance with uncertainty and fear smiled, it was a warm smile, something completely foreign to me over the past few years. I attempted to show one in return, but my face was so unaccustomed to such an action that I probably looked to him like I had recently ingested a laxative. He laughed a jolly laugh, maybe it was Xmas I thought to myself. He laughed a laugh that resonated from the soul; my hive trembled at the unfamiliar noise. I was relieved.

"It has been a long time my friend, you obviously don't recognize me." He remarked.

"No I can't say that I do." I responded.

"James Harden, we didn't speak much during boot camp but I remember you."

I was glad that one of us knew the other, but as he spoke the years melted off his face and I could see a younger James, one that talked about what he would do with all the riches he would make on this mission. He had an eager naïve face that people took to instantly. Born with natural charisma, he led without asking for followers, he dreamed and welcomed others to join him in their fulfillment.

"Now that you mention it I remember you as well, you've aged, sorry, but I half expected to see someone exactly as they appeared in my memory." I admitted.

"I understand most of us have not been able to grow old together and become accustomed to those changes a face gradually undergoes with time." He said, soothing the disappointment that I felt in myself.

"I wonder how I must appear I haven't seen my face in... I can't remember how long." It was a question as well as a remark, and James took my lead.

"Time has treated you well my friend, besides some speckling of gray in your hair you do not look a day older since last we met." I smiled, a genuine smile, one that came surprisingly easy considering the difficulty I had experienced earlier trying to accomplish the same feat. James responded with one as well.

"I have made you a meat ration as well in case you were hungry, then we can talk over what happened to me today."

"You're very kind my friend but didn't have to suffer for my comfort, I will have to return the favor on the day you are without." James said in a considerate manner. That being said I went to retrieve the rations from the warming tray and grabbed utensils for our feast. We weren't provided with duplicate utensils for our dining convenience, it was a killer on dinner parties. It was Their intention to prevent such activities. They wouldn't want people gathering together because that is when conspiring occurs. So James and I shared a knife, and being a good host offered him the fork and I ate with a spoon.

We reminisced of our younger days, days of bliss, days of ignorance. We laughed at the fun that we had during boot camp. As the night progressed we spoke about how we were being treated, and the injustice that plagued or new existence. Words that seem to make such a difference at the time but are never heard. It was a night of escapism. Escape from our prison, and misery. That night James saved my life something that I'll always be grateful for.

There were moments of awkwardness, and anticipation. We had yet to discuss what I had found earlier that day. I think we avoided the topic because it would have cut our vacation from reality short and remind us of where we truly were. James reluctantly broke the silence, with as much tact as possible.

"So what did you find today that made you rush up to me and almost scare me to death?"

I actually hadn't really looked I was too excited about having someone over.

Easter Island

"I don't know I thought I'd save it until you got here to bring it out." I sat there staring blankly at James until he remarked.

"Well let's take a look."

"Of course." I darted up and went to retrieve the mystery that brought us together.

Once I located the object I returned carrying it so carefully I must have looked like a mother with her new born. James looked into my hands, and remarked.

"It's just a rock"

"I don't think so." I said defensively. "Feel it. It's too light to be a rock and it's a weird color too."

James replied skeptically.

"It looks like a dirty rock to me."

I realized that James hadn't seen the ivory portion of the rock that my machine must have chipped away. When I showed him, he got excited.

"Do you think it's a precious stone? Let's see if we can wash it clean."

We went into my sanitation area and scrubbed away at the surface of the object. It's amazing we've become so advanced as a race but I still had to do dishes every night. It came in handy that evening anyway.

James and I cleaned the object as best as we could then we were left to admire our work. It was a smooth object, one that looked almost too familiar, in the cleaner spots it looked like an ivory chess piece that lost all its distinguishing features many years ago, a forgotten soldier that had fallen off the battlefield.

"I don't think it's a precious stone." I said with some disappointment. I never really believed that it would have mattered even if it were. I couldn't imagine being compensated for the find. There would be some astronomical price for the appraisal, or I would just be told it was a rock, while They dug mines and became very rich back on Earth.

James had suddenly acquired a very grave look. I thought the change of demeanor must have been that he had come to the same conclusion.

"You're right it's not a precious stone."

We were silent for awhile. It didn't feel like awhile it felt like an eon, it's amazing how long time seems to take when accompanied by awkwardness.

"I'd like to take this to a friend of mine to have it looked at."

The statement half surprised me, I suddenly felt like I wasn't the only one who James had enjoyed a pleasant evening with. I was engulfed in the jealousy of a schoolboy when the girl I fancied has been kicking the shins of another boy in the playground.

"You have friends?" I asked not doing a terribly effective job at hiding my disappointment.

"Of course, we meet, talk, most of all we're trying to figure out a way to let the people back home know what is happening to us." I was stunned, my heart started to race, being the natural coward I thought I was endangering my existence by having this guerrilla soldier as a dinner guest. They could break in any moment and drag us away for conspiracy, maybe even kill us for our offence. James smiled.

"Not all of us have decided to become reclusive."

My heart rate dropped and a sense of guilt came over me. James' comments made me realize that I had just lay down and died, given up. The comment hit me hard.

"It just feels like we're trapped in such a hopeless situation." I appealed to James hoping that he would assure me that things were contrary and we would find our way back home soon.

"The only thing that makes a situation hopeless is if you decide to give up hope."

It was profound, in a Zen type of way, or maybe it was just pointing out the obvious to someone who had his eyes closed for a long time.

"Okay you can have whatever it is, but you must promise me that you'll keep me informed and introduce me into your circle of friends, I think it's time that this reclusive gets out a little more." I said bravely, surprising myself at the foreign tone of voice.

"Great, it's nice to have you back." James said smiling, then instantly became somber signaling that it was time to talk business.

"I'm going to give this to my friend Thomas to have a look at, he works in the same sector that I do."

Now I had a name to accompany my future acquaintances.

"I don't think I remember a Thomas from our training."

"You're right, he came with the second wave, he was a doctor back home."

A second wave I thought to myself, I didn't realize that our population was growing, I started to gain confidence in our roles as rebels, but still I was confused.

"I'm confused, first Second Wave? And if he was a doctor at home why is he here?"

I asked hoping that James would clarify.

"Our number has been growing steadily over time there has been six waves of workers that have arrived, this is a big planet, and there are bound to be more. The search for allies just becomes more global, which makes things difficult for us. There are language barriers, so the different waves can't communicate with each other, it's all very strategic. Thomas is an American though and yes he was a doctor but he was an alcoholic first, he led a tragic life and had given up hope, that's how he ended up here, but I will let him tell you his own story when you meet."

'When we meet', I think this was the first evening that I had talked about the future since boot camp. I am now going to have doctors for friends and fight for a humanitarian cause. Things were changing very rapidly; I was going to end up being a hero after all I thought to myself.

"When are we going to find out what Thomas has to say about our find?" I asked.

James beamed at me.

"Well friend I know you used a food ration on me, there is no way that I can let you get away with that. You'll have to come to my hive for dinner, that way you won't starve a day, and I'll be able to tell you what Thomas thinks of your find."

Satisfied with his response we relaxed and the night progressed, as it would have at home, Earth.

After I got directions to James' hive we talked of the past, home, what we missed, the things that we would do differently when we got back. The evening went like this into the next day. We parted company when we realized we would suffer the next day. A noticeable drop in productivity by two workers might tip Them off. We exchanged pleasantries and the evening ended a success.

The next day I worked harder than I ever have in my short existence. It wasn't because of a new hope that had been kindled in me. I had a different type of motivation, my life. I worked as if my life was at stake. I worked hard to ensure that They couldn't notice a drop in my productivity.

After that day the days started to slowly melt into each other once again. I began to fear that maybe I had imagined my dinner with James. We had been here so long, so long that I began to convince myself of the possibility that I was losing my mind and the whole thing could have been a hallucination. However, the hope of its reality kept me going, as the time approached for me to call upon James to return the favor of dinner. The anticipation of that day grew in me the closer it approached. With each day my heart seemed to acquire an extra beat, until I was sure it would explode inside my body, causing me to collapse with a dying belch.

Finally the day arrived. It was the longest day of work I had ever experienced. Time seemed to be moving at an all time slow. Even the simplest tasks seemed to take twice as long. It was like being caught in a dream where no matter how fast you try to run it just slows you down more. The day did come to a close regardless of my suspicion to the contrary, and I made my way home.

Chapter 3

I cleaned myself like I was getting prepared for a second date. I always thought the second date was the most important one. Don't get me wrong the first date is the first impression. The one where you realize if the person sitting across from you shares the same hopes and dreams that you do. But the second date, that is when you begin to see the truth about the person. Was it really them? Or was the first date just a practiced dialog that had no reflection of the true nature of the person. I was always more nervous about the second date, being conscious of this phenomenon.

As the time approached for me to leave for James' house the more my heart began to race. The anticipation had subsided and a new sensation began to stir in me. The coward in me appeared again. It never really left; it just took control when my better judgment had deserted me. Some people have an angel on their shoulder providing insight, acting as a conscience, me on the other hand; I had a sniveling coward striking fear into me. As a conscience is to an immoral act my coward was to a potentially dangerous situation, I had always chalked it up to self-preservation.

I had never left the hive before, not outside of work hours. What if They caught me, would They kill me? Torture me until I told them what They wanted to hear? I realized I hadn't even devised a story just in case I did get caught. It was much more difficult to create a story in my new home. People didn't go for walks, or to the store. People were given their rations and worked all day, hard labor. Exercise was not needed, we were all in good physical shape, and being here and lasting as long as I did was a testament to that. People couldn't take a stroll to appreciate nature; there wasn't any. There was nothing to see. Finally it hit me; I knew exactly what to say. There was someone trying to get into my hive they were banging I jumped into my suit and rushed outside. The person saw me and began to flee. I pursued thinking that it might be a thief or even worse a rebel. That would inspire admiration in Them, it might even get me rewarded. But it wasn't enough to just devise a story, I needed evidence, there was a chance that they would not believe me. I pulled on my suit and went outside.

Outside I looked for the sharpest rock and then I began to smash it against my hive. I hit the hive with enthusiasm. My body shook to a rhythm that emerged from the banging. It felt like a tribal beat that I imagine would have been heard on the continent of Africa back home. When there was still jungle. I hit the hive again and again, and I became aware that I was salivating at an abnormal rate. It became overwhelming. I was destroying a piece of Them. A blood lust came over me, I could've killed at that moment.

The realization of my anger struck me with a wave of fear. A kind of fear I've never felt before, which was odd. I was always afraid. Afraid of the dark, afraid of being left alone, afraid that I would not succeed, afraid of what other people might think of me, afraid of pain, afraid of being discovered. But this was the first time I was ever afraid of myself and that made me more afraid than I'd ever been. I ran back into my hive, I ran as if to get away from myself. Afraid of what that thing inside me would do to me, and if it would resemble what it did to the side of my hive. I ran, through the multiple doors, into the sanitation area, I had to see myself just to make sure that I was still myself. I ripped off my helmet, plugged the sink and ran the water, every hut had a water generator. As soon as it got to an acceptable level I turned the water off. This is how I had to steal a glimpse of myself. I liquid image of familiarity that shivered with the ripples of water. I knew that as soon as I pulled the plug I would go down the drain in a whirlpool that would suck me in to oblivion.

The reflection was familiar, a face that I have known for many years. There were many changes I hadn't seen occur over the years, but the face continued to be familiar. However, despite the familiarity it felt as if there was a stranger looking back. We moved in complete synchronicity, I tried to get my stranger to make a mistake. He didn't, it was me, watching a me that wasn't entirely recognizable, but nonetheless it was me.

I began to calm down, and the familiarity of the face in the reflection started to return. I placed my helmet back on and decided to venture out again to see how bad the damage was that the stranger caused. When I came to see the power that emanated from the vandalism I was envious of the stranger. The damage was rebellious, passionate, and powerful, something that I hadn't attached to myself for a very long time. It had to be the work of a stranger. The damage did serve my purpose so I was grateful to the stranger because it did provide me with the excuse I needed to corroborate my story if I was picked up for being out by Them. The realization that I was keeping my host dawned on me, and not wanting to be rude I began my journey to my friends abode.

Traveling from one spot to another was very different in my new home. In our suits it is always silent so there is no sound other than the rhythm of your own breathing, and the sound of your thoughts. There is nothing to smell other than the stale air, that your suit would continuously pump. This was the first time I had ever noticed it. Working, one was usually in too much pain to notice that there was no sound of the machine running, no scenery, no life. When the workday was done one was too exhausted to think about their current situation, and the things that were taken for granted back home. You would just be glad the pain was over, and lie in a half comatose state dreading the work call that would always arrive sooner than anticipated. Today I realized the inability to use my senses, the ones that Mother Nature provided. The ones that aided the survival of my kind before we built our society, and destroyed our world. Fear of being discovered was what led me to this realization. As I stealthily crept closer to my dinner date, I listened for anyone following. But all I could hear was my breathing, and my thoughts reminding me of what torture I could be put through if I was discovered, I tried and strained to hear things, but my breath getting louder, I couldn't hear over it. I tried to hold my breath so that I could hear the outside world better, but ears were filled with my racing heart, beating, my head throbbing. As I walked I saw shadows race, and dart before my eyes, there was always an image licking the corner of my eyes that would playfully disappear whenever my head turned to see it. Shadows were shapeless, but in my current situation they took form, the form of my fears. I saw them hiding everywhere, in the corner of my eyes, beyond the point that I could make out clearly, around the next bend. But They were never there, They must not have been, I was never prevented from arriving at my destination.

   I arrived at James' accommodations, still afraid, I almost broke into a sprint to pound on the door of James' hive, another minute would be torture outside amongst Them, the shadows, with only my fears to comfort me. However keeping my composure I approached the door, as I got nearer I saw to my surprise the door open. I hadn't seen a door open since home, many years ago, and it had been a long time since I had seen a door open on Earth as well. Childhood was my earliest recollection, in the neighborhood that I had grown up in. Or at least began the process of growing up. My mother would leave the door open when I would come home from school. It was convenient too I remember I used to race through the rows of identical houses. The houses that stood as a monument to the Earthly dream of debt, and ownership, which resulted in one being owned. I used to barrel through the open doors to receive my reward of a sweet for completing another day of brainwashing at the local center for "education". Cynicism aside I looked back fondly at those times, those memories, those met, those feelings. Come to think of it I looked back fondly to my destitute situation back home, the one that prompted me to sign up for my life of oppression on Mars. However a door open here was unthinkable, impossible, the atmosphere wasn't even breathable yet. Maybe James knew I was coming and left it open for me just in case he wasn't present to hear my arrival, there was a second barrier that prevented the noxious atmosphere from seeping in. However, I could not look at the open door without experiencing an ominous sensation.

Whenever the human mind is in a potentially dangerous situation, the mind rationalizes it. It's the only way for the mind to give permission to pursue the exploration of a situation. If the mind was sure of the danger then the body could not put itself in that sort of danger. Even in suicide there is the rationalization that the danger of death is better than the current situation whatever it may be. I remember it was like the rationalization of a door shutting, a window slamming shut, 'it's just the wind' that's what my mind would tell me nothing to worry about. I knew there was something wrong as I approached James' hive even though I wasn't prepared to admit it to myself, I knew there was something wrong. The vacant door reminded me of a gaping mouth screaming in horror, the horror of some unthinkable act that it was forced to witness. I had to go in, I always cursed characters in horror movies for walking into such a potentially dangerous situation, but I found myself drawn to the mouth, which had now become a vacuum sucking me in.

Chapter 4

I entered and discovered the second door was open as well, this was not good, I did not take off my suit; I didn't want to die of asphyxiation. I knocked on the wall as a substitute to the door as a token act to warn anyone who lurked within, or to let James know I was present.

I crept through as silently as possible, in my suit I could not hear, or speak. I was a silent observer to my situation, it actually felt like I was watching a horror movie and this was the point that everyone knew a cat would jump out of a ludicrous hiding place scaring everyone in the theatre even though they knew it was going to happen. It was the first time a hive seemed so large. I knew it was no larger than mine was, but I saw a hiding place everywhere, nooks, and closets. I explored the living area thoroughly, then the sleeping area, I was alone.

A sense of relief came over me. James wasn't there, which meant he might have still been alive. I tried to think of what could have possibly made James leave without closing the doors, what could have made him rush, why would he have done that. Then my heart sunk I saw the door of the sanitation area closed. I approached cautiously. I knocked, there was no point I couldn't hear an answer in my suit and I knew that if there was someone in there they were probably not in a position to respond. I opened the door and as it slid open I saw an angular object that lay broken, it wasn't human, it wasn't James.

When I activated the room's illumination I saw a James I had never seen before. He was in a position a breathing man could never be in. His eyes were blank his mouth was open, filled with a swollen tongue one that made his neck swell. This was not totally foreign to me. I had found bodies in this condition in the field. For some it was how they ended their misery. The image, the emotion, the horror all swelled in me. I was moved to nausea. I regurgitated in my helmet, and then the noxious fumes made me regurgitate repeatedly. I ran to the inside door of the living area and closed it. As the door slid closed I removed my helmet as quickly as possible before drowning in my own vomit or dying from toxic air, for a moment James' fate had appealed to me. I sat down to compose myself, why would James kill himself, it didn't make any sense. James was expecting me to come over for dinner that very night, so why would he kill himself.

Answers ran through my head: because he couldn't take it here anymore, because he couldn't take another night of my company, because he wanted his body found before it began to deteriorate. But I realized none of these reasons could be true. I knew I wasn't the greatest of companions but even back home no one had ever gone to this extreme to avoid my company. James was full of hope for the future. He talked about the great things that we would accomplish. Then I realized it must have been Them. They must have killed James and made it look like suicide, but why?

They must have found out about his association with the freedom fighters. They might be looking at me right now, I, by coming here, must have been found out! James' fate awaited me next. But then a realization came over me. My heart began to race but with different result. I was not afraid. I half wanted Them to burst through the door, after I got my helmet back on of course, so I could punish Them for what they had done to James, my friend. James died before I had a chance to lose him as a friend, before I had a chance to disappoint him. James died my friend. They robbed me of hope, of happiness, and of a friend, and They weren't going to make me afraid any longer.

I visited James, when I entered he looked like James again, uncomfortable, but James none the less. I cried, and hugged him for the final time thanking him for resurrecting me. I turned my back with thoughts and aspirations clouding my mind. How was I to continue my fight, to enter amongst the freedom fighters? James was my link and I had just lost him. Then as I took a final glance around James' hive I noticed a note, one that was my pass to enter the boys club again, it read: Thomas "the link". Coincidence I thought not, it was fate, and it made me brim with confidence that I was to have hope, and happiness, and friends again.

I cleaned my helmet side by side with James. It would be the last thing we ever would do together. After I was done I left his sanitation area to be his tomb. As I walked into the living area I snatched the note and a meat ration from James' cold storage area, and left, leaving the door open behind me.

Easter Island

Chapter 5

The walk home was a much different experience. The fear of shadows and the time that seemed to stand still when I first left for James' house was gone. Now I dared the shadows to be one of Them, or all of Them.

The shadows shrunk back in cowardice as I strode through them, confident, head raised, eyes set to meet any challenges. I was home in minutes compared to the hours it seemed to take my first time around. I noticed the gash in my hive, and I looked at it with pride, I knew that stranger, I liked that stranger who looked at me from the dancing water, I knew I would see that face again. That face was me, and this time I would not spiral down into oblivion. I entered my hive and took off my suit. I sat and glanced at my trophy, the note, and began to plan how I would find Thomas.

I didn't know where he lived, what he looked like, or what sector to find him working. I knew that the only way to get into contact with Thomas was to get noticed by Them.

The next day at work I realized in my pool of sweat what I had to do. I threw down my machine and waited. When the conformity probe made its rounds I knew it would notice me because I wouldn't be registering enough body heat for its sensors. Just as I suspected when the probe made its rounds it stopped and its lights flashed, it was actually very ornate it would have revolutionized Xmas decorations. I picked up my machine accordingly and as the conformity probe seemed satisfied with my response to its light show I playfully clubbed it like I did when I played tee ball those many years ago when I was a child. The probe lay in a crumpled heap and I waited for Them to arrive.

It didn't take long before They arrived, acts of public disobedience and rebellion had to dealt with swiftly lest it become contagious. They looked as They always did, indistinguishable from each other, indistinguishable from us. That was the most fearful thing about Them, They looked the same so it was never certain whether They were Them or us. They were invisible but Their threat was always present. The only marker that would give them away was Their emblem. It was sewn on Their right chest and each shoulder. The emblem was angular, symmetrical, cold without feeling. The emblem had come to represent what I imagine what the swastika had come to mean to the Jews of the early twentieth century, an emblem to this day abhorred. However, the emblem was not something that could easily be picked out from a distance, it usually meant that if you saw it you were in Their possession. I was quickly apprehended and didn't resist. I knew this act would put me on the path to Thomas.

They painted my visor so I would be blind. There I was conscious, blinded in the hands of my enemies, a nightmare that I could not awake from. However, I was unafraid I welcomed the passing time as it only furthered my goal. Occasionally there was a prod, or I was jostled. I fell often. Trying to negotiate uneven land without sight is not an easy task. While down I was trampled then violently propped up to feebly move ahead before I fell again. I thought that they must be enjoying themselves, it all seemed like a game. A game that may have been played in the school yard while a gang of boys kicked and tormented another who may have been different, a quality always punishable with cruelty. We finally arrived at our destination. I could tell because I walked in to a solid object and when I regained my footing after a few steps the ground flattened. After a few steps my helmet was removed.

I was in what seemed to be a hangar; it was huge, ominous, and very active. There was a constant rustle of activity like mice burrowing, except there were no mice here, and I doubt they were brought for the trip. I guess it would help battle homesickness, but I doubt that They had any feeling at all. No it rather made sense that Their activity reminded me of mice for I felt that They were all rodents of some type.

I couldn't see anything beside my escorts who had decided not to reveal Their identity. They took me to a door, a very solid door, one that did not bode well for escape. It was solid metal and looked as if it was taken from a submarine from back home. I thought that I might not find Thomas after all. I couldn't if I was locked up in this prison.

Then I thought that my stay in my new cage wouldn't be a permanent one, it couldn't be, if it was They would have just killed me, it would have been easier. I knew They had plans for me I just didn't know what, one thing I could count on is either way I would find out. After They opened the door I was less then gently introduced to my new accommodations. As They left They shut the solid metal barrier, imprisoning me alone with nothing but darkness to keep me company.

Darkness, again surrounded in darkness, from blind to blind I had continually been unable to see, unable to see the truth, unable to see hope, unable to see the future. I had finally awoken from my slumber, my cowardice, and They had tried to keep me blinded. Time elapsed, that's all I could decipher, but that's a given, I couldn't approximate how long I was in my tomb because time was not perceivable in my state. Time can be measured from event to event, sleep to consciousness, work to relax, and meal to meal. All was the same in my state there was no event to measure anything against.

Finally I heard the door to my tomb creak. Light flooded my space blinding me, painful light that blinded me more, from blind darkness to blinding light. Incapacitated I lay motionless watching the apparitions dance before me, hoist me up to take me into the light, the painful blinding light. They did not speak They just were present prodding me forward clasping my shoulders so I could not fall. I moved forward, I could feel the space surround me. I was taken into another room, I heard the sliding of a door, and always the scurrying of mice. I was thrown into a chair strapped in and abandoned by my escorts. I was left with only one apparition. One that peered into me, the shadow got closer then moved, and again moved closer and moved away. The shadow moved about busily, jars rattled, focus started to return to me, as did my shadow, it was human, features started to become perceivable, and then another light flooded from above. I felt as if I was being grilled in a police interrogation. The painful light blinded me again, and then I felt a sharp pain in my neck, accompanied with pressure, fitting how the perceived became literal. My shadow had attacked me. Maybe I was now a guinea pig for Their tests. I was overcome by a blissful euphoria and I began to sing.

"Me and my shadow…"

My companion was not amused, or didn't appear to be.

"Friday, I promise to give you just the facts, and only the facts."

Still silence, this shadow was a tough crowd.

"What's a matter don't rodents have a sense of humor?"

I didn't really expect an answer, but I didn't much care for one anyway, I didn't care for much of anything. I heard the door again They must have returned, I wondered if I should try my material out on my new audience. Word must have gotten out that I was in town, I must've been a better draw than I had thought. But this audience had something else on their mind. I heard a muffled thud and murmuring, it was the first time I had heard voices since arriving. Again I was hoisted up.

"On the road again…" I sang.

I was abruptly stopped with a sharp pain to my mouth. At that moment I thought it would be better not to act like a drunken vagrant who had been given the microphone at a Karaoke bar. Liquid warmth filled my mouth, one that had to be relieved. I spat a liquid that continually replenished. My audience seemed to worsen.

My act had become much more interactive than I had hoped. I decided not to proceed and took five so to speak. Barley on my feet my audience began to prod me again, still shadows, my eyes couldn't focus, the pain in the neck did not help I am sure, nor did the unfamiliar surroundings or the light in my face for so long. We were on the move again probably to begin more uncomfortable probing, I becoming more convinced that I had become a guinea pig for Their sick experiments.

However, if I would continue to be in the state that I was in currently I couldn't imagine that I would mind that much. I heard the sliding of the door and knew that we would be on the move again. I began to stumble forward suddenly I felt one of my escorts plant what felt to be a shoulder into my stomach, the action not doing wonders for my equilibrium prompted me to collapse on to my playful friends shoulders. At that point I was hoisted up and we then began to move. Since I was given a lift I thought it would be best to enjoy the ride, I relaxed letting consciousness slip away.

As things became distant, the burrowing of the rodents, the nauseating motion my vision slowly began to come into focus, and I caught first sight of my escorts. As they faded I saw faces, human faces. It was a great disappointment, I half hoped that they weren't human, it facilitated greater hate. I let it all fade to black and decided to wait until I was awakened by some sort of probe that was inevitably going to rudely awaken my slumber burrowing into a place that probably was not meant for entry.

I wasn't rudely awakened. I awoke in darkness, I thought I had been returned to my abode prior to being given my narcotic. I thought it didn't make any sense that I was drugged not tested, or interrogated, it just seemed pointless. Unless the throbbing headache and nausea that I had were just a torture method that They had designed. I thought I could get used to this kind of torture, heck I used to pay to do it back home in my younger days. I realized though that I wasn't returned to my cell, I was warm and comfortable.

I was lying on something soft and covered by something that engulfed my whole body. Maybe I was being tested, I thought that maybe if I moved I would experience some sort of pain, or shock or if I tried to remove my hand from my casing I would be disintegrated.

This could have been some sort of incarceration device. I decided to test it, I moved, nothing, I removed my hand to expose it, nothing, I completely threw the covering off of me, nothing. I reached down and felt the covering, it was soft and puffy, it was a blanket. A blanket

I thought to myself? I now knew that I wasn't back in my cell.

A chill came over me and I pulled the blanket over me again. For some reason it had a very soothing effect, one of protection and warmth, I wondered what Freud would've said. I didn't understand what was happening so I lay quiet trying to understand my situation, attempting to dissect it. However my head was throbbing so hard that it was difficult to keep a train of thought together, let alone think. I decided to clear my head and not worry, I knew it would all be revealed to me in time. Then I heard it, I heard something foreign to me for many years, I heard laughter, distant but close. I heard the murmur of conversation, I didn't hear burrowing, I didn't hear Them, I heard us. At that moment I knew I had arrived.

Chapter 6

I struggled to my feet; my equilibrium was still off from the narcotic I was given. I tried to move forward but my feet couldn't firmly plant themselves. I was walking on the cushioning. It reminded me of my youth going to camp jumping on beds with other children, but it had been so long and felt so foreign that I toppled over and fell back into the cushioning. I let out a giggle as I hit the cushioning, and quickly covered my mouth. I couldn't help the giggle it was like the whole experience tickled.

    Knowing what to expect I thought I'd make a second attempt at rising, this time I was more successful. I maneuvered my way to solid ground. The hangover kicked in. As soon as I hit solid ground the room started to spin. I toppled over again hitting the ground, and this time there was no giggle. But determined as I was I staggered to my feet once more and began to follow the murmur of voices. They got louder as I moved closer using the rough wall to support myself as I walked. I got close enough that they sounded like they were right beside me. I saw a glimmer of light and I knew that was where I would find the source of the voices. I plunged into the light. It was a bad move. The light flooded into my eyes like two hot pokers piercing my eyes. I fell again.

As I hit the ground I saw shadows rushing to me, it was like the shadows were dancing. I heard a rustling of comforting words from all sides, things like "Careful no need to rush", and" Don't worry you're safe now" all in different voices, I began to weep. I heard one bark "Get him back into the dark he isn't ready for the light yet". I felt myself get lifted and I was returned to the darkness, but this time I was not alone, some stayed behind.

There we were in the dark, a group of us, just like it was a slumber party after our parents had told us to turn the lights out. It was awhile before someone broke the silence.

"Bet you're in some pain, I remember when I first arrived it took me three days before I was comfortable in the light."

"Where am I?" I asked the shadows

"Safe" was one reply.

Someone commented "You think you could be any more specific John?"

I smiled.

"I can't help it if I have a flair for the dramatic" was the playful reply.

"Yeah you rank up there with the Shakespeares of the world."

"Considering present company I can't help but agree."

I hadn't heard that kind of playful banter in ages. It reminded me of high school smoking sessions of one-upmanship. I felt safe regardless of its dramatic implications, and was far too weak to participate in the fun. I was afraid that I was also rusty at these types of games that I would only embarrass myself anyway. I became used to rhythmical throbbing of my head and slipped from consciousness, hearing the entertainment slowly drift in the background.

That night, or day, I couldn't really tell, I dreamt dreams of youth, strength, convictions, and an eagerness to embrace the future.

I awoke rejuvenated. The past few days had flooded me with images of the past. This had made me see myself for the first time in ages, had made me feel old feelings that I thought I would never feel again, had made me think of things that I hadn't thought of in ages. Yes, it was a time for the ages. I couldn't help feeling that I was in a viscous circle experiencing and re-experiencing things that had lied dormant for so long.

It was a continual period of awakening. It was like a dream that one has where you dream that you wake up, but it is still a dream, and it keeps repeating until you actually awaken. The funny thing is that when you wake up or dream that you wake up you believe that you are awake. This occurs repeatedly until one cannot be sure whether they are truly awake or not. This is what I felt always that I had experienced an awakening, one that was final. I then would experience another, and I always met it with surprise.

It was happening so often in the short time span that I began to be unsure of my awakenings and suspected that there was always another waiting for me around the corner. Never sure if I had fully awakened from the long slumber that They had lulled me into.

I still catch myself experiencing awakenings, awakenings that allow me to see with more clarity. It is the part of the maturation process that They had robbed me of. They had stagnated my growth. The wave of progress I made returning to human interaction was dizzying. But I was beginning to feel more like me, hope was returning, pride, I was undertaking the journey of self-affirmation in spite of Their attempts to prevent the destination from being reached.

I was still in darkness. I had to stop myself from leaping up and bounding into the light lest I wasn't ready yet. I didn't want to suffer the same pain that I experienced the first time around. I opened my eyes and adjusted to the lighting, or lack of, before I took the next step. I began to make out heaps of blankets, it must have been Their issue, jagged walls, one's that looked as if they were reaching out at you threatening, menacing, like an old knotted tree that was unable to bear leaves. But I wasn't afraid, an image that would have typically conjured up the coward in me was actually welcoming, they were reaching out to me, these walls were in pain, and I felt I could heal them. I stood up and placed one hand over my eye. I remember learning that from an army movie I had seen back home.

It was a trick used by soldiers on the midnight watch. If a flare had been ignited by the enemy, by covering one eye, the light from the flare wouldn't steal you're night vision. I figured I might need it if I couldn't handle the light. This time I didn't hear any laughing, there was only silence. I made my way toward the light. I thought to myself about 'entering the light' and the advice in all those stories, television shows, and movies about how entering the light after death was making one's way toward heaven. I knew I was still alive because the light that the shows I was referring to allude to is always beautiful, this light was painful.

When I emerged on the other side, I smiled. I was alone, and very disoriented. I reeled from the pain that the light brought on, but this time it was bearable. Colors and images glowed, there were no boundaries, colors blended into each other. It was impossible to distinguish one object from another. My mind, fast at work, attempted to process what items it could. An item's location, color, and size made it possible for me to begin recognizing my surroundings. A table surrounded by chairs and a deck of cards lying complacently on the tabletop. In a different section there was what looked like an area for another game drawn in the dirt, with pebbles for pieces. There were no floors the walls were rock and the ground was dirt. Actually more like dust, the layers and layers of dust that was on this planet, dirt would have moisture, which would mean water, which would mean life. I thought how odd it was that we were here, on a planet that obviously didn't want life. I didn't think it was odd that They were here They were never wanted, anywhere.

I was alone. I wasn't sure what to do to occupy myself until my new roomies would re-emerge. Luckily it wasn't long before an opportunity for activity made itself available. I heard burrowing noises, it was the sounds that They make. My heart started to race, what if my new roomies had been found out, slaughtered and now they're base of operations was being inspected. What would They do to me if They found me, I would be slaughtered for sure. I thought of ways to escape, I could beg for my life:

"They kidnapped me I'm not part of them, I tried to tell them that all I wanted to do is return to work, but they wouldn't let me go, thank god you arrived to save me from them," I would plead.

I thought that would work, I heard my voice pleading in my head, I hated that voice. The burrowing got louder.

Maybe it wasn't Them, maybe it was one of us, I hoped, my heart felt like it would explode.

I saw a shadow dance on the wall, it was a cold mechanical shadow, it was Them. It came around the corner and it noticed me, Their emblem prominently displayed on Its suit.

I dropped to my knees, the tears welled up in my eyes, I don't know if it was out of fear or shame. I looked up to see It, as I moved I felt the tear run down my cheek and neck hiding from the confrontation under my clothes, I wished I was a tear. I looked at It, me on my knees and It looking down. Our eyes met, sure I couldn't see past Its visor but I could feel the contact between us, I could feel Its loathing, Its superiority, my anger.

I leaped to my feet; it was an action that surprised both myself and It. I lashed out at It and struck it on the helmet with a force that was strange to me. I felt every bone in my hand crumble with that blow, and I smiled, I liked the pain, welcomed it, I wanted more. It stumbled, I'm sure out of shock; I couldn't have hurt it with my blow against Its suit. I seized the opportunity and threw It head first into the cold solid rock wall.

The coldness colliding against each other made a hollow ring throughout the cave. It was music. Its body hit awkwardly, and the body lost some of Its rigidity. I climbed on top of It to rip off Its helmet. They worked pretty much like ours. I unlatched it from Its armor. As I tore the helmet away I heard laughing. It slowed my anger. I raised the helmet to smash It into oblivion. I took a final look at It and It was laughing as well. Suddenly a surge of people rushed in, laughing.

I heard various comments on what just occurred, I felt multiple slaps against my back, I was lifted to my feet. It got up smiling at me, It embraced me, and I felt the pain as the various broken bones swam in the swelled pool of my once recognizable hand. It wasn't long before it was submerged in liquid by the resident medic in attempt to subside the swelling. I was lost in confusion, weeping of relief, happiness, and uncertainty. I saw others weeping through smiles and laughter. They must have shared a similar experience that was relived as they watched me. Finally some semblance seemed to begin. People started to take seats in the dust. I could still hear the murmur of people discussing my experience like people used to talk about a heavyweight boxing match back home.

"Did you see that punch"

"Those were some pretty nice moves"

"Too bad it wasn't really one of Them, there'd be one less now"

"Lucky we came when we did otherwise Geoff would've been meat"

The murmur began to subside. Someone began to speak,

"As you know when ever we attempt to add to our numbers one must face a test. This test is a rite of passage into our company. However, it is a test not meant for sadistic pleasure, not for selfish amusement, or childish hazing. Although I feel that sometimes it is viewed in that way by all but the participant."

His tone was parental and disapproving. He continued,

"No our test is one of survival. We must test prospective allies to ensure that we are not admitting one of Them into our ranks. By using Their attire it tests whether the prospect is one of Them, or one of us. I remind you all of the time when it was one of Them, who tried to lay plans to sabotage us.

"It was eliminated. I remind you all of the many times that it was one of Them because their fear made them submit to their oppressors. They had to be returned. But every now and then we do find one of us. One who will risk life to be free, one who cherishes their individuality, one who embraces death rather than a life oppressed. Today we welcome one, one of us, one who makes us more, one that makes us stronger, one that we add to our one cause, one that we know will die for us as we would for him. Let us welcome our one, who has demonstrated that he belongs with us and deserves our admiration."

The cave echoed with cheers, defiant cheers that were unafraid of discovery. I felt the walls swell with the sound of unity, I felt at home. They began to chant:

"Speak, speak, speak, speak" I felt a warm whisper tickle my ear.

"They're talking to you."

I rose and the cheers began again like a wave that almost staggered me, but I was caught in the undertow of emotion.

"Hello" I humbly began. My audience returned a resounding "Hello".

"I have been here many years, slowly dying, I was one of the firsts. I was promised fame and fortune and was delivered anonymity and oppression." I was surprised at the ease in which I was delivering my speech. "I was like many, afraid to do anything, afraid of my oppressors, and not convinced of my worth, that I may have deserved to be oppressed."

The audience grunted, and agreed, in the sympathy of a shared experience. "I had died, my whole life I was dead, but here it was Hell." There was a swell of acknowledgement. "I thought I deserved my Hell, at least didn't deserve better, I had stopped dreaming, hoping, and began to be the machine that They wanted me to be. That was until James arrived. James and I came over together. You all must know James because he told me of you. He made me hope again, dream again. But I was still too afraid of Them. They had seeped into my blood. I needed to be exorcised. I was to meet him, but when I arrived he was dead, slain by Them. But when I looked at him, he was beautiful in death. Not like the others that die in the field and die empty. They die like machines. They get run down and just stop working because they were lifeless to begin with. But James was alive and in death he was beautiful because his life was beautiful and his memory was beautiful."

I heard some tears in the audience, those who must have known James. "It was James who revived me, who helped me find the me that had been buried. I was reincarnated by his death, and he exorcised Them from me" The audience began to sporadically clap and cheer. "It was James who revived the dream and it is through me that James' dream will be realized. My name is Elijah and They will learn my name, They will fear my name, because it has strength, and because it has numbers. They will not stop me for I am James' dream, that which cannot be slayed for it is already dead, and continues to live, if not in me, in others. We will exterminate Them. Exorcise Them from themselves, and rid Them of this planet like the plague that They are. Claim this planet for us because we have built it, it is ours, and let them know back home that we are here, we are fine, and we are reborn." Cheers erupted, this time it did stagger me. I looked into the faces of my audience through tear soaked cheeks. These were not tears that wanted to be hidden. Tears that would crawl down your neck and hide under your clothes. These were tears that wanted to be seen. These were tears that weren't ashamed, or were cried out of shame. These were beautiful tears cried out of self-affirmation. I saw the same tears from us. I looked in to each of our faces and I saw me, and I saw strength, and I saw home.

After the gathering rations were distributed. We ate, talked, and laughed. I spoke superficially with many. They mostly welcomed me, spoke of my fight with, I gathered his name was Geoff, Geoff thanked me for not killing him, and complemented me on my speech. I was overwhelmed by the amount of human contact that I was experiencing for the first time in many years. But mostly I grimaced because of the pain of my hand and its many bones that once fit together. I thought to my self 'all the kings horses and all the kings men' my hand was a puzzle that needed to be put together again. But this was not the time for pain. The meal finished, people broke off into groups and then someone approached me.

"Elijah, let's take a look at that hand, you've been favoring it all night and after the blow you dealt Geoff I wouldn't be surprised if you broke something"

I agreed and followed my newfound physician. We entered a room that contained an area for rest, a table like structure for examination, a chair, some lights, and a collection of various jars and gadgets against the wall.

"Take a seat on the table Elijah"

I leaped on to the table.

"We will have to give you a proper physical soon, but there isn't much point with all the crap that's been pumped into your system recently. However, in the meantime let's look at your hand."

I stretched out my arm to display some wretched part of me that was once usable. I looked at this foreign piece of me, discolored, disfigured. I felt the pain throbbing through my veins. My physician erroneously touched it. I shrieked and pulled my hand away.

"Are you crazy, don't touch it!" I said, stupidly hoping that it would never be touched again.

"Why is it on display? I don't believe you went through feasting without asking for help. If you ask me you're the one that's crazy."

He reached back into the assortment of jars and pulled out a gadget. He then carefully took the contents of a jar and inserted it into the gadget, which he was obviously planning to use on me against my will.

"Give me your hand Elijah" He said calmly.

"No" I replied defiantly.

"I'll give you three reasons to give me your hand: one you'll probably never be able to use it again if you don't. Two I'll touch it as often as possible, and three I'll tell every one in the company that you want to shake their hand, and only the right hand."

The humor helped, I was being childish. I held out my hand and turned my head. I felt a prick in my hand and then a warmth that engulfed it. The pain disappeared. The physician continued.

"I'm going to wrap it up, and hopefully it will heal, we can't really operate here"

The physician wrapped my hand. I closed my eyes. When he finished he said.

"There all done, you've been a good boy would you like a lollipop?"

I smiled.

"Thanks Doc but I'm trying to watch my weight for bikini season, by the way what's your name?"

"Thomas."

The name was familiar, I said as much.

"I was a friend of James' so I appreciated the speech, he was a recruiter on the upper ground so we didn't really know what happened to him. When you told us of his death, it was the realization of what we all already knew but could no longer avoid."

I replied.

"I remember now, I had a stone I found, and James said he was going to give it to someone to analyze, he said his name was Thomas. And when I found his body I saw a note that read: Thomas the link. The same Thomas I presume?"

"You got it Elijah. So it was you're stone, I thought it was after your speech. But Elijah it isn't a stone."

"What was it?" I asked.

"It's a bone."

"So it was probably from one of the workers on the upper ground" I explained, as a parent would to a child who has heard a strange noise in the middle of the night.

"It couldn't be." Thomas replied.

"Why?"

"Because I've dated it to being thousands of years old!" I could hear his excitement in his whisper, I was silent, we were silent.

"Are you sure!" I exclaimed.

"Well I can't be a hundred percent sure" Thomas began to explain, "I only have a basic understanding of radiocarbon dating, and I could only put together a crude imitation of a radiocarbon dating machine with the various scraps I have found on my surface excursions. I like to tinker with technology to try and learn as much as possible about this planet for science's sake."

Thomas had a hobby I thought to myself, something that was unheard of on this desolate planet. Thomas continued:

"I always thought that this could be an incredible leap in our understanding of the rest of the universe, that's partially why I came. But it took only a short time before I realized that it is an opportunity not being utilized by Them. But I wasn't going to let that stop me, the fact that They didn't care about discovery gave me more reason to. Anyway the radiocarbon dating machine is supposed to measure the decay of the radiocarbon isotope in organic materials. The one thing that I can't account for is the rate of decay that occurs in the material. I know on Earth it depends on the amount of solar activity, and the concentration of radiocarbon in the atmosphere. But here the atmosphere is so much weaker so does that account for quicken decay or is it prolonged? Was Mars' atmosphere always this weak? If not when was it strong and what was its composition? There are so many questions to be answered, but by my calculations this bone is either hundreds of thousands of years old or it is from last month!" Thomas paused for effect. I was amazed and remained awed in silence.

"The reason I believe the former is that a bone couldn't be this shape, or this polished without the aid of some years of erosion, but then again you never know what They might be doing to us when we're captured or to those in the field who become unproductive. But still the rate of decay just doesn't seem right"

"It seems" I began slowly, almost cautiously, "that this new home of ours has many mysteries yet to be discovered, mysteries that require investigation. But now is not the time, now is the time to take this planet for ours and rid ourselves of Them, then we can begin travelling the road to discovery".

"I agree, I think James thought that this bone chip was the piece of the missing link in the chain of human evolution, the fact that he left a note saying as much has convinced me that's what he was thinking".

"Well what our find tells me for certain is that this exploration of Theirs is not one of discovery, or science, it is one of economics, and if James is right then we're home".

We talked Thomas and I at great length that evening, and by the morning we were friends. I slept in the rest area of his infirmary. Thomas fell asleep in his chair. When I awoke I thought of us all being Martians and how the green men on Mars did exist, it was Them and the green was money.

Chapter 7

My life began with the freedom fighters with much optimism. But it didn't take long for me to recognize that we were simply a group of subterranean pranksters. We'd kidnap hopefuls from the surface, commit random acts of vandalism, and thieve the supplies we needed from Them.

They were never really threatened by us because we never tried to commit an act that would prevent Their machine from functioning. We fooled ourselves into thinking of ourselves otherwise. We spoke of being the exterminators and ridding ourselves of the infestation of Them.

As time passed our numbers grew. Growing in number made sustaining ourselves much more difficult. I think the rationale was that if we took their workers one-day we would be more than Them, but They just kept importing new parts to the machine. And we just had more mouths to feed. The spirit of our company began to wan. We became stagnant I had to speak. I can't remember the exact night or the exact words but I remember that it was time to take a look at ourselves and decide what we were going to be.

We had a choice to be a subterranean league of rats, that would be exterminated as soon as we became a burden enough for Them to bother. Or we could start the revolution. We could take this land that we worked for. We could free our fellows from Them. It was met with approval by the masses, I noticed I was becoming much more of a speaker, much more of a leader.

But how to ensure that my words weren't wasted fodder to subside the feelings of unrest until it reemerged again? I had a plan, one that was building ever since my arrival. We had compiled maps, a huge assortment of maps that leaded to all Their compounds. We had tunnels leading to all of Their compounds for our supply raids. The element of surprise was in our favor. The tunnels were cold and dark, but breathable. We were able to travel to each lair without the need of suits as well as penetrate Their lairs without our suits.

Each had an artificial environment. The tunnels, from what I gathered, had an artificial environment due to their interconnectedness with the lairs. On our raids we only took what we needed, and we only took food, and people. It was hard to do anything more, we had found a way to survive and escape oppression.

That was enough for most of us. But not for me, James' death affected me. I did not want his to be a death in vain, an unjust death. I had already seen too many unjust deaths go unpunished, it was my excuse not to live and become a shell. I felt that if I let the same happen with James I would die again.

I wasn't going to allow myself die again, plus I had half humored James' theory of the missing link, I liked it, it meant that we had come home. The new home was where I was reborn, and I wanted to help breathe life back into the dead planet. My hand was healed, it never looked the same but the pain was gone and I could use it. I had begun to participate in the raids. I made sure the next one would be different.

The next raid I was responsible for acquiring a quarter of our rations. But I had an ulterior motive. That night Francis was lead. He was a kind man who knew everyone, he was a good lead because he always cared about everyone, and would ensure their safety. To that end he was very cautious as well. People didn't disobey his lead out of guilt, he wasn't a strategist, and that we all knew. I didn't care though. When we emerged from our tunnel into Their lair, you could immediately hear the burrowing sound.

But it was always less when we raided, either in a time of patrol for a certain lair or the lair was in a period of rest. They were always guarded but we just raided sporadically enough that it was hard for Them to plan for our strikes. It was amazing that we had avoided a real confrontation for all this time. We would sometimes encounter Them but would always retreat, we never engaged in a melee.

Their burrowing sound always made me think of how our roles reversed. Now we were the rats trespassing in the lair of the rats, I wouldn't trade it for the world. Francis had called for the strike but I broke formation knowing I would get the look later. I looked back at him when I broke formation and he already had the look, he couldn't say anything though because we functioned under complete silence.

Easter Island

It was part of the agreement with Them: we pretended that we weren't there and they gave us food. I had theorized where the armaments were kept from the maps that we had, and I was going to test my theory. When I arrived at the location it was guarded. It made sense they'd let us survive but not get strong, or desperate. I wouldn't be dissuaded. The dead me would've whimpered and retreated pathetically with tail tucked between legs.

This incarnation of me was different; I stealthily pounced on the lone guard. It wasn't expecting the need for attention since nothing had ever happened but that had just changed, and it would mean that I had to make this hit count, because guards would now be on alert. I quickly was on top of my victim, it was over in a swift motion: helmet off then crush the skull.

The fate that Geoff had so narrowly averted. I entered the armament and grabbed everything I could, not knowing what anything really did I took anything that looked interesting, like a child on a shopping spree in a toy store, grab everything and then figure out what you have afterward. The trick was to grab from the right location, this looked right, or that felt right. Only time would tell if it was right. I loaded up and converged with my group, they just stared in amazement at me. Francis wore a look of horror on his face, it was better than the disappointment look, I didn't feel guilty. We dove into our tunnel and proceeded back to camp. No one talked to me. There were only murmurs and whispers of question. Francis was silent. It would be his last lead.

When we returned I went directly to the feasting area where we always gathered after a raid. It is where we displayed the booty and reported any loses or casualties. Usually a group returning from a raid was received with cheers, but this day was different. I entered the area and was met with silence. It was broken by the cold clang of the artillery that I had pilfered. Francis, and company, followed behind, and it was Francis that spoke first.

"We have returned with only three quarters of the rations required."

The audience groaned, and all eyes fell on me. I felt the weight of their glare.

"I am responsible"

I chimed, the audience became restless and the whispers began.

"I broke formation, I went for weapons."

"Explain your actions Elijah" a voice rang for the audience. It was Seth. Seth was a leader among us. There was no head, or president, or chief, we were a family, people didn't require to be thought for, the needs were expressed commonly and people volunteered in turn. But that never prevented leaders from emerging, some people had the natural ability to motivate, to make decisions. Seth was one of those people. He was the one who spoke on behalf of the group to welcome me to my new family.

"It was time" I replied resolutely.

"It was time for what? Time to get us killed? Time to starve?" Seth began to scold.

"No," I interrupted forcefully "it was time for change, it was time to start doing what we believe in, it was time to act."

Seth interrupted "Act on what, what do you believe in Elijah? Suicide? Starvation? Who will starve Elijah? We will not be a quarter less in numbers this month. Do you believe in suffering Elijah? Because that is what you've caused."

All eyes returned to me.

"Yes, Seth, I believe in suffering it is all that I have known, it is all that is here. I don't want to live like this. We talk of great deeds. Well great deeds are always accompanied by sacrifice, and I will starve."

"So will I!"

"I as well!" rang voices from the audience, the weight of guilt began to lift.

"Will you die as well?" retorted Seth.

"What is death to one who does not live?" I replied.

"We live Elijah that is what we do, we rescue the oppressed from the surface, we house and clothe many, we live equally, do you want to risk that?"

"Seth, you are asleep, we survive yes but like vermin, we burrow in the crawl space and come out at night to steal our food, that is no way to live." I explained.

Seth was not convinced. "You're mistaken that is exactly our way to live it is how we have lived for this long, why would we risk giving that away?"

"We risk giving that away every time we grow in number, we are larger and hungrier, and require more and more, as soon as we affect Their bottom line They will exterminate us like the vermin we mimic. Do not be fooled, it is our fate, I do not accept that fate, I choose another one, one where we are free. It is time," I continued "to lay claim to our land and exterminate the infestation of Them."

"Elijah if you condemn Them for treating us like vermin doesn't exterminating Them like vermin make us Them. How is this unlike the witch-hunts back home, Hitler and the Jews, the KKK and the African Americans? Each believed in their superiority and committed atrocities because of that belief?"

"We are not superior, look at the state that we live in, but there are some fundamental rights that are worth fighting for, the right to not be oppressed, the right to make choice. I want to exterminate Them, not people. I want to rid this planet of Their influence. Those who want to convert will become us."

"And if They don't?" Seth was quick to interject.

"Then They die, and They die by choice. Have you looked outside Seth, have you seen the killing fields. Our fellows are killed on a whim. If weakness is demonstrated it is as good as committing suicide. The suicide! Think of all our fellows who have lifted their helmets to escape! You are right Seth it was wrong how Hitler, and the KKK treated their victims, and those who died trying to fight them died honorably, they died for something worth dying for. But remember Seth They are the Hitlers and the KKK, we are the victims of Their oppressions and atrocities, it is time to end this atrocity, it is time that we act. To confront Them, and we can do it on Their terms, or ours. Do not fool yourself Seth They will come one day, and if we are to remain like rats we will be just as easily exterminated. I do not relish that moment, I will not be squashed like a simple bug, I wish to stomp back."

Cheers met me and the weight of guilt was lifted further. But Seth stood fast.

"Death is ugly who ever wears its mask, and you have made the decision to dress too many of us tonight. You robbed us of our freedom tonight, you robbed us of our choice, you were the oppressor. You cannot tell the future, They might have never come. I do not know if I choose to live by your decisions, and I feel this requires further discussion on how we are to act. We are a group here, and we should decide as a group. Tomorrow let us discuss as a group what our next actions are to be."

A general wave of agreement passed through the audience. I agreed. But it had been done, and the seed had been planted. Our group started to divide. Those who agreed with Seth, and those who agreed with me. I saw death in both sides, impending death, and death met with honor.

Luckily we weren't divided long, in the end the decision was made for us.

The next day I arose to chaos, people running, crying, the air was alive with shouts of,

"It's not fair"

"They're dead you know"

It took Seth, myself, and some other respected members of the group to corral everybody and gather them together in one area. It seemed that three member's of our group were passing through the tunnels when they were ambushed by Them. Our fellows were defenseless, surprised, and slaughtered. They made the decision for us. It was no longer open for debate.

Easter Island

Chapter 8

It is a funny thing about human beings, anger produces adrenaline, adrenaline produces aggression, aggression produces violence, and violence enables revenge. The once peaceful man is turned to an animal in less time than it takes to realize his anger. It is purely chemical. The deaths were on my hands, I killed them with my decision, I had to accept that. The question was, how do we respond? War had been declared. They would let us live as long as we remained weak and not an economic burden. When I stole the weapons I had given us power, a power that couldn't go unnoticed.

We debated our next actions as a group. We were all in agreement that we were now in a state of war. It was time to strategize. We decided to seal the entrances to a large portion of our tunnels. They were too cumbersome to always have guards posted. We did guard our entrances at one time, but as I understood, we kept finding more portholes to Their world, and since They never bothered to enter ours we began to not post watchmen. We became comfortable with Them, and it cost us life. We sealed all the entrances to territories that didn't contain all our needs, which now included weapons. With our extensive collection of maps we were able to theorize which camps had all our needs, the rest of the entrances to both our worlds were sealed with the weapons I had stolen. We had very limited weaponry, only enough for one man to carry, it was not enough to fight a war. Our first goal was to find, and gather as many weapons as we could. We had become quite good at hiding in the shadows, and conducting our raids. Now we brought weapons, and took weapons, and took lives, Their lives. The group became quite proficient at killing. Thomas began to teach medicine to those who showed an aptitude, the wounded began to pile up and it was far too much for one man to handle. Seth and I led platoons, along with others. Seth and I became the source of strategy. We used the maps to decide where to hit, every so often we would seal entrances and open others. It gave us the edge in surprise, and it worked like a charm.

  The war was long, many people died on both sides, as with any war. Thomas was one of the many fallen, I concluded that his initiative to train others in the art of medicine was not because he couldn't handle the volume, but in case he wasn't available. I learned that there wasn't much Thomas couldn't handle. Some say that life is too precious to waste for the sake of war, but when you fight for life, death is never wasted. All fought with courage and pride and when one fell it gave us strength. We grew stronger the longer the fatality list grew, it became a mission not to disappoint the fallen's memory. Not to let their deaths be a waste, or forgotten. They kept coming though, there just seemed to be an endless line of faceless, lifeless machines. We continued to battle, our extensive maze of tunnels seemed to be impossible for Them to navigate, we would sometimes come upon Their corpses frail and lifeless, those who got lost in the tunnels and couldn't find Their way back. I could understand how They got lost, I sometimes got lost, we had more tunnels than maps, but I was familiar enough with our maps to find my way back, even when in uncharted territory.

 As the war wore on work on the surface ceased and They were faced with anarchy. They couldn't fight a war and oppress workers at the same time it became too cumbersome, and the workers began to revolt, and fight, and kill. They were attacked from both sides from the surface and below. They began to diminish in number, and then They stopped coming. Their number diminished, and was not being replenished by more machines, I guess They gave up and decided to stop wasting resources on us, it must have been rather costly. They decided to protect Their profit margin instead.

We had won the war, but not without the loss of many a friend. I could tell many tales of battles fought in the trenches, of friends made and lost during the course of battle. However none would end on a happy note. And to properly pay homage to those friends found and lost, and those battles fought whether in victory or defeat would take a lifetime to tell. So much happens in war that the events of one day can take weeks to explain. I will not demand such a commitment from my listeners, nor undertake the burden of immortalizing those lost by some exaggerated portrayal. People do horrible things in war. My life is a testament to their memory, not a telling of it. In any event after Their evacuation the remainder of Them were eliminated with relatively no casualties, and we celebrated. We celebrated many days and nights and reveled in life, and freedom and mourned those who weren't able to see this day. We wept for joy knowing that they did not die in vain and that this war was one of worth. It was funny, how all this started with a bone chip, a very old bone chip, one that was the catalyst to the freeing of the slaves. That bone was the catalyst to my metamorphoses, and I was the catalyst for our victory. I took pride in that and felt regret for the deaths I caused. Our planet became our large playground. We explored how They lived we slept in Their stations, it was like sleeping in coffins of the absent dead. We tried on Their armor, we crawled in to the skin of our enemies and walked a mile, we walked many.

I explored the tunnels, I was fascinated by them, there was so many, their walls of Martian rock that felt so foreign yet familiar. I found that there were many tunnels that hadn't been mapped. It confused me that so many had existed, that so many led to an opening. I asked one of the elders, one of the original freedom fighters, we could truly call ourselves that now, about their existence. He shrugged,

"They were always there, and they always led us to where we needed to go."

The answer confirmed my suspicions. I first became suspicious when I realized that there were more tunnels than maps. I initially thought that they were linked to Their lairs, but there were more tunnels than lairs. I then began to think that the tunnels were a result of some kind of natural phenomenon. A phenomenon like the Grand Canyon back home, but that never explained the fact that we had the ability to breathe freely while traveling through them. I spent many days of my freedom exploring them, and their mystery. They always took me to some new strange world, a world of dust and rock, but it was always new dust and rock. Finally, they took me somewhere special. They let me in on their beautiful secret.

I had opened one of the portals to new dust and rock, placing on my helmet before entering my New World for the day, but when I had gone to touch the walls, as I always had on my travels, I noticed something. There was a blemish in the surface, one that seemed to travel in a pattern. I started to feel the walls all over, noticing that there was in fact some pattern, it felt almost like Braille, I started to dust the walls with vigor, my excitement became more and more climactic as I felt the mystery unfold. My enthusiastic dusting left me completely engulfed in a cloud of red. I stood back to let the dust settle. The rock and I were one, indistinguishable from each other, both red. As the dust fell to the ground and on my suit I saw the truth, and then I didn't.

I awoke on the ground lucky that I didn't damage my oxygen generator. I had fainted. I scurried to my feet to see if it was still there, and not a mirage, Mars was one large desert after all. It was still there, in all its magnificence, a collection of carvings. They were intelligent, not luck, and they were familiar, yet undecipherable. The designs seemed like pictorial carvings on the wall. Put together in various sizes of v shapes, or wedges. It was definitely the work of a being with motor skills. I spent hours sitting in front of the masterpiece bonding with its beauty. I felt like I was in the caught in a portal of time, a liminal state. I was transcending worlds, space and time to experience what felt like another culture. I always fanaticized about coming in contact with other worlds, alien cultures. The fantasy is always that we meet, interact, with human like beings that we can learn from, fight, or be enslaved by, not all these fantasies are happy ones. Human beliefs are a product of our media, literature, and fables after all. I found it odd that I might have made first contact with an alien culture, although it seemed like a contact with ghosts.

After many hours I tore myself from the wall of carvings and thought I would share my findings with my fellows. Upon arriving back at our camp I attempted to share my find with the rest of the group. I was brought back to the memory of finding the bone chip and my excitement I tried to express with James. But this time I could speak, at least I thought I could. I removed my helmet, and when I began to relate my finding I stammered and shook with excitement. My audience was half-afraid that something horrible had happened and half amused at the spectacle of me. I couldn't speak no matter how hard I tried, and I just continued to get more excited and frustrated. I could sense my audience felt as much. I couldn't believe that I had become that blithering idiot that was so annoying in all those movies back home. The one who would try to tell a group about an axe murderer looming behind them, but could only make distracting noises, and humorous faces that only aided the axe murderer by causing enough of a diversion that the axe murderer could go unnoticed. They tried to console me,

"Calm down"

"What is it you're trying to tell us"

They would guess feebly, and I felt like Lassie. Finally I was approached by Geoff, he looked at me, our eyes met, and he struck me with the back of his hand clear across my face. It was a sharp slap, one that actually made the noise 'slap' obviously how the action had acquired its name, and it was a forceful slap one that introduced me to the ground rather quickly. In any case it worked wonderfully, I had fully re-gained my speaking faculties. I knew because I cursed Geoff immediately. Geoff helped me up,

"I've been waiting to get revenge for your first day for years. Imagine all those television shows we saw where a slap stifled hysteria actually worked, who says TV isn't a great education medium."

"Thanks, " I replied "I don't think I could've managed without you"

"Don't mention it, I could give you another if you think it would help?"

I declined his kindly offer.

I was finally able to relate my findings and I watched my audience's faces as I told my story. I could read their faces, as they must have reflected mine. We were a mirror to each other, surprise, disbelief, awe, excitement, fear. There were many questions,

"Do you think that means who ever did it is still here"

"Maybe it was just Them who did it"

"Can you take us there"

The final question I could help with. The whole group came, and anyone we met on the way we absorbed, I felt like the pied piper. When we arrived I could feel the amazement on their faces, I couldn't see their faces through their suits but I knew it was there. All that I had brought stared in wonder it was obvious by the way they all stood silent and motionless. One member of the group became overly excited and began feverishly waving his arms. He was trying to tell us something but his suit was a field suit and he could not communicate with the rest of us. Again I saw myself when I had first approached James with my original find, the bone. It was futile, we tried to show him that it would have to wait, and then he pulled some of us back into our tunnel where we could breath once again. He was like me when I first fell upon the group stammering and pathetically trying to express myself. It was like listening to your voice on tape. You knew it was you but it made you uncomfortable to witness it. I learned from what was effective once and slapped him, I did it partially because I knew it would work, and partially to punish him for showing me how foolish I must have looked when I first came back to camp. He cursed me as well, it was Desmyn, a jovial intellect who was everybody's friend and was so genuine. He started,

"I know that writing!"

"You do?" rang a chorus of us.

"Cuneiform, it's an ancient writing system that was made with wedge shaped objects! But what is it doing here?"

"Can you read it?" I asked.

"No," Desmyn replied, "but I may be able to figure it out!"

His response gave us hope. It turns out that Desmyn studied Anthropology in University, and as there were not many opportunities back home for his knowledge. He had found his first love and wouldn't leave her, but the world shunned him for his choice of a mate. He had told me over the weeks that followed that it was the reason he was here, he half hoped that he would find something like this, but never truly believed it would happen. We told Desmyn that deciphering would be his sole responsibility.

When word had gotten back to camp, there was excitement every where. The carved wall almost became a tourist attraction for us. Everyone wanted to take a look, or touch. It also brought out a rash of volunteers to help decipher what the carving represented. It turns out that we were surrounded with linguists, ancient historians, and anthropologists. The castaways of Earth because they provided no value to a society based on science and technology. It was ironic that they were our scientists now, exploring, attempting to uncover the truth, and that a scientist would be of little value to us, at least in this endeavor. The work began and we waited, patiently, impatiently, our lives revolved around their work until Seth had made us turn our attention to more pressing needs.

"We are all going to die." Seth calmly addressed the group one evening.

"Why Seth do you share such joyous news with us this evening" was my reply to Seth. Seth and I were of opposite nature but had a profound respect and fondness for one another nonetheless.

"There is no food."

"No food!" was my shocked response.

"Not now," Seth clarified, "but soon, and there is no means of acquiring more".

Seth was right it was a reality we had overlooked, in our bliss we forgot about reality, how were we to get rations if They were not here to receive the supply? Seth was being responsible by reminding us of our priorities.

"What do you propose?" I asked. I knew his answer but I thought it would be proper for me to give him the appropriate segue-way.

"We cannot cultivate the land, we were working on creating an irrigation system, not farming. We have no seeds or enough of a water supply to begin cultivation. In any event nothing would grow fast enough to feed us all, and nothing would provide us with enough nutrients to survive either, nothing that we could grow here anyway. We must leave and return to Earth".

There were groans of disappointment. I jumped to Seth's defense.

"Remember," I said, "it was our goal to return home and spread the word of the crimes that our oppressors had committed. Make Them face charges for their crimes and give a voice to Their victims".

"How will we get there?" were the responses to Seth and I. Knowing Seth had thought about this prior to mentioning it, Seth would never begin a discussion unprepared.

"There are plenty of ships that were left by Them, in the coming months we must learn them, understand them, for they are the only means off this planet, and they are the only means to avoid death."

"We don't know how to fly or anything about spaceships, we were brought here from poverty" was the general reply, I continued for Seth,

"There are plenty of mechanics in our ranks, people who know machines, we must learn and use those aptitudes".

"Who will fly them?" they continued skeptically.

"Do we have any pilots? Anyone with a pilot's license, anyone how has had flying experience?"

They consulted; some stepped forward.

Easter Island

"I dusted crops," yelled one.

"I flew commercially," yelled another.

We had two, which equaled hope and enough to get our next endeavor started. We left those in our group who were working on the carved wall to continue their work, we only stole their manpower when required.

Easter Island

Chapter 9

People worked around the clock, and the sense of urgency heightened as time passed. Our food supply was quickly diminishing, while the demand for food grew. Labor tended to demand more sustenance for the body, but the supplies weren't there, and it became obvious that if we were going to make it, it would be close. It made it difficult on us, we were hungry, and the constant pressure of starvation looming over us caused us to argue more, fights broke out with greater frequency, and the overall moral was morbid. We were working for our lives, without any reassurance that we would be successful.

The resources were distributed to make sure that there weren't any blemishes or weaknesses in the shell of the ship that may cause any malfunction. The mechanics investigated most of the machinery to try and understand how each part functioned, to ensure that all equipment was both functional and if not could be fixed if the need arose. The electricians checked wiring to make sure that none of the wiring had eroded from previous journeys and that every thing was 'plugged in'. We had other laborers do various tasks like ensure fuel levels, search for fuel and food by scourging the empty lairs. Our first glimmer of hope turned out to have disastrous results. We achieved the ability to test a ship.

    The commercial pilot had been working endlessly to figure out the controls. In the beginning the crop duster and the commercial pilot worked closely together, but their inability to see eye to eye about what the various knobs, levers, and buttons did resulted in their parting of ways. We thought that we had made progress, ready to test the ship and we still had minimal food supplies. The commercial pilot confidently boarded the ship, and prepared for his role as hero. The engines initiated wonderfully. The ship rose majestically like a sunrise, the dawn of a new day, and new hope for us. As the ship climbed into the atmosphere it wavered, and we held our breath.

    It looked like an angel that flew too close to the sun, and as soon as it reached its apex it plummeted. We gaped in horror. The shipped plummeted so fast that the screams didn't escape our mouths until the quake of the impact was beneath our feet. Then a groan could be heard, we mourned for our would-be savior's life as well as our own. We were left without a completed ship, a crop duster for a pilot and food that wouldn't last a week.

Faces were long, there were feeble attempts to boost morale. Various individuals remained positive, but overall the outlook was bleak. Regardless we continued to work. Our crop duster motivated the ship workers as best he could. He believed that the only error was that of the commercial pilot's interpretation of the panel functions. His position was that if we could get the ship into the same state we would be fine until we had to land. Not words that inspired confidence, we were told that we could get up but not down, and we had all witnessed what could happen if you got down wrong with our loss of the commercial pilot. Still we worked, we knew what had to be done, so investigation work wasn't required, but there still wasn't much time.

On the third day since we lost our commercial pilot, and begun the work on the second ship we ran out of food. It caused a panic throughout our camp. There was a rash of suicides of those who would rather die quickly than starve. This meant fewer laborers, and more time was required to complete the ship. We worked without food as long as we could, but the hunger pains became too great.

On the tenth day we began to eat the remains of our fellows. The atmosphere or lack there of, made it impossible for the body to decay. We used the machines that would tear apart the surface of the planet to tear apart our departed friends. We stored the smaller portions in the cold storage of our hives and the empty lairs making it possible to eat our fellows frozen. The bodies did not rot, and no life forms were on Mars so there was no worry of any bacteria that would infest our comrades remains, this meant that we didn't need to worry about sickness. It didn't prevent a rash of nausea amongst us. The first time it never stayed down. The thought of what we were doing was often enough for the body to reject the food.

However, it was also difficult to keep the food down as our systems became so accustomed to no food that when food came digestion was difficult. The final problem was going from our rations, of synthetic proteins, and food compounds to authentic meat. None of us had eaten real meat in years, and it didn't always agree with us. The difficulties compounded when not all of our number would eat the remains of our fellows. There was a moral principle that they would cling to. We were divided, and they would die for their principles, while we just wanted to survive. We watched them die, and when it came time we would consume them.

We would leave them to the last because we know it was against their wishes to be eaten, they were our fellows after all, but they knew their fate would be food if it came to our survival or the wishes of the dead. It is terrible to watch someone die of starvation. You could see the body feed on itself in an attempt to survive. The flesh became sunken as the body took all it could from the body to survive. A starving person's stomach swelled from the volatile intestinal acids.

It was an odd sight to see a starving man with an exaggeratedly huge stomach. Still though it was a stomach on a skeleton and it didn't look healthy. After some time it wasn't uncommon for one to go blind, lose control of their bodily functions, and lose their mobility. They died on principle, and we watched the suffering that can be associated when one clings to their beliefs. We had accepted our need of survival, and didn't look at it as anything other than that. We were animals who required sustenance to survive, and we fed on what we could. I will never forget those that died though, it was very human of them to do so.

They were more human than us, we were more animal, the human in them was able to conquer the animal to the point of self-sacrifice. What I will truly never forget is that they continued to work through their starvation as long as they could, in an attempt to aid the cause of escaping our grave. It was either their hope for survival or their hope that they could still help us in our mission to escape, in either case they were saints, Seth was among them, led them.

On the twenty-first day since we lost our commercial pilot, and begun the work on the second ship a discovery was made. All were in the gathering area consuming, when Desmyn rushed in minus his breath. We all stared at him waiting for his breath to grace his lungs. His eyes told us that he had news. As soon as Desmyn caught his breath he began,

"We know what the wall says, it was a language, one of our linguists cracked it two weeks ago, since then we've been piecing it together."

"Well what does it say" came from the mouths of more than one intent listener.

"It seems to be a history, or a story, of the previous occupants, would everyone like me to tell the story from the beginning, it may take awhile?"

"Yes!" was the resounding response. Desmyn's discovery was the first thing that had taken our minds away from our compromising position; it was a welcomed distraction.

Easter Island

Chapter 10

Desmyn began his tale of discovery, "Well the writing on wall begins by talking of the greatest civilization, one that lived in peace, one that lived in paradise. They must have been technologically advanced because it discusses buildings, automation, and manufacturing. It seems that they became such an advanced race that the typical challenges that are faced by beings were overcome: child mortality, hunger, wild animals, etc. But their population grew exponentially, so large that their environment became too overwhelmed to sustain them.

They knew this was a threat so they had begun looking for new homes, and ours is one that is mentioned. However, it seems that whenever they attempted to cultivate land and settle their population large 'monsters', or 'dragons' destroyed them. This, we assumed, were dinosaurs. The dinosaurs posed a difficult problem for them. They came equipped for war, but their enemies were to fast, ferocious, and many. Any expedition that traveled to Earth was never heard from again.

Years were spent on devising a solution to overcome this problem. In the meantime, limits were placed on children that families could have, food production was annexed by the state and distributed 'evenly' throughout the population, and criminals were put to death, regardless of crime, this was done in an attempt to balance the population problems. It seemed to be successful in the short term. Meanwhile, their scientists constructed a weapon that would eliminate the dinosaurs.

The weapon would be launched from their planet and hit the surface of the earth. The weapon would release a chemical compound that would react violently with the dinosaur's respiratory system. This solution posed a problem for them however. Although the airborne chemical would kill the dinosaurs the impact of the weapon would fill the atmosphere with debris. This resulted in an ice age caused by the inability of the sun's rays to penetrate the atmospheric debris.

This made the planet uninhabitable until the ice age subsided, meaning that they would have to wait. Their short-term success at managing the growth of their society and its resources led them to believe that this was their best solution. However, as time passed it became difficult to maintain such a rigid, form of government and society.

The government officials in charge of collecting the food became more militant in their responsibilities. Farmers became more reluctant to give up their crops for the 'greater good'. Rebel farmers fighting the government appeared. The government food distributors became corrupt, hoarding for themselves, and giving extra to those who could afford to pay.

The people became hungrier, and restless. The rebel farmers became difficult for the government to manage. Civil war ensued between the government and the farmers. The army soldiers who repelled the uprising made more demands on the government to fight. The government helpless to their demands had to submit. They gave the soldiers extra food, money, what ever it took to appease them." This kind of power in the hands of soldiers had always spelled disaster to society. Desmyn's story continued.

"The soldiers abused their rights, and continually asked for more. The farmers were removed from being a threat, either in death, or in slavery. The government had become a military state. Corrupt soldiers overshadowed the previous problem of corrupt governors. The rules of government, like food rationing, and population limiting were forgotten in a generation, and the society began down the path of rapid self-destruction once again.

It seems the military state lasted for generations, it was a period of much violence and confusion. Various generals would claim power over the army and attempt to rule the planet; however, with so many different generals vying for the same title there was much murder and changes in leadership. The actual soldiers would support any general as long as they continued to reap the rewards of their support. Finally, the living conditions became perilous. Food supplies were at a minimal.

Earth had not become ready to inhabit, and without the planning and strict living conditions imposed by the original leaders, Mars had become uninhabitable as well. Animal life and vegetation had disappeared. This was the result of the population consuming at far greater a rate than animals or vegetation could be replenished. The manufacturing of synthetic foods lacked in various areas of nutrients that were required to survive.

Easter Island

The general populace blamed the soldiers for their suffering, the soldiers blamed the generals, and chaos ensued, violence in the streets, mass murder. The end result was that this sophisticated society spiraled into chaos, there was images of rape, patricide, matricide, parents killing children, siblings killing each other, the tradition spread for generation until killing became a way of life, it was almost like mass insanity.

People cannibalized for food, much like us, it was the only method of survival, and all were the hunted. Finally a group of tribesmen converged to make peace. An agreement was reached where the council of tribes leaders whose names read: An, Inanna, Enlil, Enki, Ninhursag-Ki, Ereshkigal, and Utu. These great tribesmen re-instituted the goal to venture to Earth.

However, to continue the race only one pair could go. The remaining resources and technology could only build a pod for two, so it would be up to these designates to continue the race, and culture in the New World. The games were held among the six tribes. Many competed to have the honor of continuing their once proud race. If victory was not earned death was the punishment.

Easter Island

This was the method that during these times of peace the tribesmen had figured to feed their members. Many died voluntarily the honor to compete and have the honor to continue the civilization of the New World was great. The games were designed to test strength, stamina, and intelligence. The games of strength and stamina were typical of our games at home; the final test was the one where many perished, a riddle,

'What goes on four legs in the morning, two at midday, and three in the evening?'

Because no one was able to answer the riddle the game continued. No one knew the riddle because the prospective initiate would only hear it when passing the other trials, and upon failure would be killed. The only people who knew where the head tribesmen.

People trained their children from birth for the question but it was never answered. This went on for years. During this time the tribesmen built these tunnels. The air quality of the planet continued to decline with the decay of their atmosphere. This was the result of the pollution that was produced during the reign of the military. They had the foresight that the surface might one day be uninhabitable, and by building the tunnels and an oxygen generator."

We all stared at each other in amazement. We couldn't believe that no one had asked the questions as to the origins of the tunnels. The generator was described as being housed in what sounded like a pyramid. The pyramid was built close to the previous capitol city of the civilization and a memorial structure that was dedicated to the dead described as the mournful mother, some sort of crying face. This was a part of the planet that we had never seen.

We must have been surviving much like the original inhabitants of the planet, maybe even breathing the recycled oxygen that once filled their lungs. In any case it confirmed that They didn't care for discovery, They only cared for profit. They must have found the tunnels, They could have found the generator, but They chose not to, or not to care which is even a greater crime. Desmyn continued with the story,

"Finally Enki had an illegitimate son named Ziusudra who had planned to challenge for the right to travel to the New World. Enki, who loved the boy, secretly told Ziusudra the answer. However, before

Ziusudra could answer the question he had to overcome the flood of other initiates. Along with the well-placed help of Enki Ziusudra succeeded to the final test. When asked the question Ziusudra answered man 'who crawls on all fours in the beginning of life, who walk upright on two legs in the prime, or midday of his life, and finally walks with a cane, a third leg, on the eve of his existence'.

Utu proclaimed Ziusudra victorious and there was much celebration. They had found the one that would give their culture, continued life, or immortality once again, and that immortality was Ziusudra. The vessel was prepared and Ziusudra left with his son Uanna-Adapa who was to be the founder of the new-world. He would be responsible for rebuilding Dilum, which is what they affectionately called their home, or what we call Mars.

That is the story, or history of our predecessors, and that is where the writing ends." Desmyn finished.

It was an amazing story. One that was all too familiar; it was the story of us, of human beings, of Earth.

"What happened next?" someone asked, like a child who didn't want the story to end, who wanted to know the details of the happily ever after.

"We can only speculate." Desmyn replied.

Easter Island

We had been left to relive their legacy or suffer the same fate of the remaining tribes. We would end up in a similar fashion and so would Earth, if we didn't get off this planet, Dilum. After the story was over we dispersed for rest. Desmyn was congratulated along with his peers and the story remained fuel for the rest of us for the following weeks. The camp was alive again and we talked of what life must have been like in Dilum before and after, we related it to our home, and we became involved with all the different possibilities that Ziusudra and his son Uanna-Adapa could have faced. The distraction of the story, and the return of Desmyn and his peers to help us prepare the ship helped the group's morale and sped up the progress of the ship.

On the sixty-fourth day since we lost our commercial pilot, and begun the work on the second ship, the second ship was ready. The toil had paid off and the lives given to the cause not lost. We had a ship, and new hope. There was to be no test flight, the camp couldn't take it if the same fate befell the crop duster as it did the commercial pilot. This was the last hope; we would all take off and land with the ship whether the landing was successful or fatal. It was a better fate than that of Seth and the others. We all prepared ourselves, and boarded the ship.

The ship was accustomed to transporting men. It had been the deliverer of Their reinforcements during the war, so it sat us quite nicely. I supervised that all were seated and took my role as co-pilot. There we were a group of castaways, a collection of mechanics. Liberal arts majors, and some others, leaderless we piled all our hopes on a crop duster who had no space flight experience. I looked at our savior, the embodiment of the crop duster stereotype. Grizzled complexion, toothless grin, what teeth remained were yellow.

He wasn't a poster boy for hygiene, but he was our poster boy for hope. He was confident and spent most of his time smiling and singing. He would periodically laugh, a hearty laugh, a laugh one has when coming to a humorous realization. Yet, he never spoke to anyone, he was alone and happy, and as most of us thought he was crazy. Feeling my discomfort in my co-pilots chair he leaned over to me, and spoke,

"Now don' worry, 'ol Earl is gonna gets us home nice n' safe."

I couldn't believe his name was Earl, we were doomed, I thought to myself.

"I knows I never flown a ship like this before, but wit all our modurn technology I figure it'll fly isself once I get it in the air, jus' follow the prompts is what I say."

I couldn't believe he talked like that, we were doomed, I thought to myself again.

"Now I know that bein' co-pilot an' all makes ya think ya have some responsibilities, but don' worry I can handle this all by my lonesome, an if I cain't than no one else'd be able to anyway, we'd be shakin hands wit Jesus before our heads hit our asses."

Then he let out one of those laughs, and so did I.

"Well here she goes, pray if you gotta god if ya don't got one than pray there is one we're gonna need 'im."

Earl began to flick switches and throw levers with surprising dexterity and confidence, seeing him perform helped calm my prejudices against Earl. The ship quivered like a delicate flower in the morning breeze. She creaked like a house of many years and memories. But most importantly she moved. We all held our breaths, which was probably wise we were unsure how much oxygen was left on the ship, we all held our breath except Earl, of course, Earl sang. The ship began to move. It rose with uncertainty, like a buoy in the water it danced up and down, and so did our stomachs. The power of the engines made the whole ship rattle, and it sounded like it was going to break into pieces but Earl kept singing, I kept holding my breath, and the ship kept moving. I must have turned four shades of blue before I deemed it safe to take a breath. Earl looked at me and remarked,

"I'm glad that you decided ta breathe I dint wanna hav ta give ya mouth ta mouth, I'd hav ta give ya my school ring afterwords."

I was also relieved that Earl was not going to give me mouth to mouth. I smiled, it was enough for Earl, and he began to sing again. The ship kept rising much to our surprise, into the sky, into the atmosphere, and into space. We had made it, and we were on our way to Earth, I began to weep. Earl interrupted,

"Now don' get too comfortable we still gotta do a hyper leap, or warp drive, or the worm or somethin' otherwise we'll die like sardines in a tin by the time we get home 80 years or so from now."

Earl always knew what to say. Earl once again began the routine of flicking switches and pulling levers, everything on the ship became silent. Earl looked at me and began,

"That's funny I followed the…" A flash of light occurred "…prompts?" And we were facing Earth.

"OOOOOEYE" Earl exclaimed, "Now that was flyin'"

I still couldn't believe Earl spoke like that I was waiting for the act to end, but I hugged him and told him I'd give him my school ring any day. Earl became bashful and warned,

"Now it tain't over yet we still gotta land, and that's the hurdest part."

Again Earl demonstrated his ability to give well-placed reassurance. The ship plummeted into Earth's atmosphere and the ship once again began to rattle. I was sure the ship was going to disintegrate along with us in Earth's atmosphere, I remember hearing that most car accidents happen within 10 miles of the beginning or final destination, I thought in respect to space travel this was the equivalent. Earl continued to sing, he yelled at me,

Easter Island

"Now I'm gonna aim this thing to hit onea our oceans because the ships gonna proally be hotter than Nevada in July by the time we get through the atmosphere."

Earl was obviously full of quaint witticisms. I just nodded and braced myself for impact. It all happened in a flash Earth, clouds, blue, then impact, more blue. We hit three or four times before the ship stabilized. The whole time Earl was busy at work pulling things, flicking things, I thought it was primarily for my benefit.

"Ya see that we musta skipped eight, nine times like rocks we useta throw at tha cottage"

I agreed, said maybe we got to double digits, through tears, I embraced Earl. Once again he was bashful. After convincing the rest of the crew that we were not dead we opened our hatch to the beautiful blue skies of earth, the glorious blinding light of the sun, the invigorating smells of the ocean, polluted air and real oxygen, not artificially produced swill, all greeted us. We were also greeted by the barrels of many weapons that surrounded an unidentified extra terrestrial object that had just trespassed into Earth's mainland. We were home.

"And this is how I have come to tell my story." The eyes of the audience were fixated on me. "We have all begun to tell it to those who will listen, newspapers, television stations, people like yourselves who are curious of the Mars, or Dilum, expedition. Many of us keep in contact; some have not and have assimilated themselves back into society in an attempt to forget. But they will not be able to because our story, their story, will reach their ears once again. Desmyn and the group that had figured out the writing of the Dilumians has gained much notoriety, he has linked the language to the Sumerian, or Elamite, civilizations of three thousand BCE.

When I heard as much I smiled at the thought of James' theory of the missing link and how maybe he wasn't that far off. The rest of us continue to speak, fulfilling our commitment to those we lost to Them. James, Thomas, Seth, and the many others who died so we could return. Their memory will live on through our stories, and their contributions not forgotten. Because our story is not just one that is to reveal the truth about Them. Our story is a warning to take care of Earth, and not throw away our beautiful home, it's the only one we have. Don't let us follow in the footsteps of our predecessors, our ancestors. Let us learn the lessons from our own experience let us not allow Earth to become an Easter Island."

Printed in the United States
2132